Stepping
Forward
Series

Illustrated by
Emily Petre

Fishing With
Uncle Nathan

By Mary Martin

Rod and Staff Publishers, Inc.
P.O. Box 3, Hwy. 172
Crockett, Kentucky 41413

Telephone: 606-522-4348

ISBN 978-07399-2524-9

Catalog no. 2887

1   2   3   4   5   —   25   24   23   22   21   20   19   18   17   16

Fishing With Uncle Nathan

Introduction

The stories in the *Stepping Forward* series are written to help beginning readers find that reading a book is enjoyable, satisfying, and worthwhile. Careful attention has been given to vocabulary and sentence length to make them appealing to a first grade student.

This series has been divided into steps. Each step is slightly more advanced, to be used as children increase their reading skills. *Step Four* books focus on reinforcing the consonant digraphs.

In the beginning stages of learning to read, some children may benefit from hearing a story read to them before they try to master it themselves. This may be done by working through the book together, page by page, or by reading the whole book to them before they begin to read. Many children, however, will not need this help, and will enjoy the challenge and satisfaction of reading the books on their own.

Because these books have been written for children who are learning to read, we encourage adults to not give opportunity for preschool children to memorize these stories, since that would hinder their value.

Giving children enough practice in reading is crucial to their mastering the art. Therefore, having them read the right books—and lots of them—can be of great value. *Stepping Forward* stories are designed to aid children in becoming good—and interested—readers. These books are ideal for independent reading by primary children at school and at home.

New concepts in this book:
- —Consonant digraphs (sh, ch, th, <u>th</u>, wh, ng).
- —the suffix *ing*
- —two-syllable words

Story Titles

1. Sheldon and Rachel
   in the North 13
2. Going With Uncle
   Nathan 18
3. Into the Boat! 22
4. On the Lake 27
5. Fishing 32
6. Rachel's Fish 36

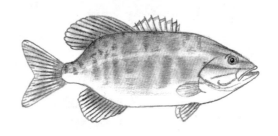

7. Sheldon's Big Fish........... 41

8. Sheldon Gets a Fish........ 47

9. Time to Go Home.......... 51

10. Finding Father
        and Mother 54

11. Fried Fish for Lunch........ 58

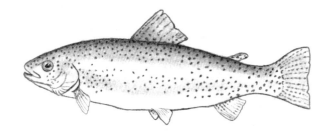

Sheldon and Rachel
in the North

"Whee! This is the day!" said Sheldon. "This is the day we go fishing! This is the day we go fishing in the North!"

The sun was coming up. The sky was getting light. It was not hot yet.

What a good time to fish. What a good day to fish in the North.

Sheldon and Rachel's home is not in the North. But Sheldon and

Rachel's family came to the North to see Grandfather and Grandmother. Sheldon and Rachel's family drove and drove for two days. They drove and drove two days to get to the North.

Grandfather and Grandmother's home is in the North. Uncle Nathan's home is in the North too.

Sheldon and Rachel's family came to see Grandfather's. Sheldon and Rachel's family came to see Uncle Nathan's too.

Uncle Nathan wants to take Sheldon and Rachel fishing. Sheldon thinks he will like fishing.

Rachel is afraid. She said, "Will we
be safe in the boat? Will we sink?"

Father said, "Uncle Nathan will
drive the boat in a safe and wise
way. He will show you what to do.
You will put on a life jacket. Then you
cannot sink. If you sit still, God will
keep you safe."

Mother said, "I hope you will catch some fish. God made fish for us to eat. I think that pike are the best fish. Pike grow until they are very long fish. I think you will catch some pike today."

Sheldon nodded. "I want Uncle Nathan to teach me to fish. I hope we can eat some fish for lunch. I wish to sink my teeth into fried pike. Yum!"

"Fried fish will be a good lunch," said Rachel. "If Aunt Judith makes fried fish, our family will like that."

"Get your jackets on," said Father. "Uncle Nathan will be here before long."

The children obeyed. Yes, they obeyed fast. The two children were waiting for Uncle Nathan. They were waiting for him to come and take them fishing.

Going With Uncle Nathan

When Uncle Nathan came, he did not need to honk. Sheldon and Rachel were watching for him. They saw his pickup coming in the lane.

Sheldon and Rachel ran to Uncle Nathan's pickup truck. Uncle Nathan will take them fishing!

Sheldon said, "I saw many lakes here in the North. To which lake will we go?"

"Watch and see. Watch and see where we will go," said Uncle

Nathan. "We will go to a lake that has many fish."

Uncle Nathan and the children drove up the road. What did they see as they drove?

They saw many, many trees. They saw big, big rocks and some lakes. The big, big rocks were like hills. Many trees grew on the rocks. They saw two deer among the trees.

Uncle Nathan and the children drove on. The children saw no sheep. They saw no steers. They did not see big sheds or shops.

What did the children see as they drove on up the road? They saw a few homes, but not many. They saw a few homes beside a lake.

Uncle Nathan and the two children drove in a long lane.

Bump! Bump! Bump!

It was not a wide lane, but it was quite long.

Bump! Bump! Bump!

"Whew!" said Sheldon. "That bump made me whack the side of the cab!"

The lane went this way and that way among the trees. What did the children see as they drove on? They saw more trees and more big rocks and a muskrat home in the water.

"A buck! A big brown buck!" Rachel's brother said. The buck ran across the lane.

Rachel asked Uncle Nathan,
"What is that—in the sky?"

"That is a big black raven," said
Uncle Nathan. "God made all these
things that we see."

Into the Boat!

Bump! Bump! Bump!

Uncle Nathan drove the children in the long, long lane. The boat was at the back of the truck. When will they get to the lake?

At last Uncle Nathan said, "I see the lake! I see the lake where we will fish!"

"Good!" said Sheldon. He had a big smile on his face.

When Uncle Nathan drove up to the lake, he said, "Children, you need to get out of the truck. I need to back the truck into the water. It is not safe for you to be in the truck when I do that. You can stand here and watch. Stay here so you will not get in the way."

The children saw Uncle Nathan back the truck into the water at the shore. He did not back into the deep water. Then Uncle Nathan slid the boat into the water. Uncle Nathan tied the boat to the dock.

Sheldon got into the boat. He was in first. He was in before Rachel. Uncle Nathan did not need to help him.

Rachel was afraid. Was Rachel sorry that she went fishing? Maybe. Maybe she was sorry.

Rachel was on the dock. She saw her brother in the boat. She wanted Uncle Nathan to help her. She saw Uncle Nathan working.

Uncle Nathan took some things to the boat. He laid two long fishing rods in the boat. Then the children saw Uncle Nathan take a box and a net. He laid them in the boat too.

Uncle Nathan got some life jackets. "Here is a life jacket for each of you. I will show you," he said. Uncle Nathan put on a life jacket. "This is the way we do it. Can you do it too?"

Uncle Nathan threw an orange life jacket to Sheldon. "Put it on!" he said.

Sheldon obeyed. The life jacket did not feel good. The life jacket felt too thick. It felt too big. But Sheldon obeyed. He kept his life jacket on. He did not fuss. He was going fishing!

Uncle Nathan said to Rachel, "Your brother can put his on. Let me help you."

Then Uncle Nathan said, "Come. I will help you into the boat."

"Come, Rachel, come! Come, Rachel, come!" sang Sheldon. "Let's go!"

Rachel and Uncle Nathan got into the boat. Rachel felt the boat rock back and forth. The waves were splashing by the boat. Rachel hung onto the boat. Rachel did not like the boat to rock, but she was brave.

On the Lake

"Whee!" said Sheldon. "Off to the
lake! Off to the blue lake! Here we
go!"

Rachel saw that her brother was
happy. He was happy to go fishing.
Was Rachel happy to go fishing?
Maybe she was. Maybe she was not
sorry she went fishing.

Uncle Nathan made the boat go.
The two children saw the waves
splash. Sheldon felt the wind in his
hair. The sun shone on the water.

Did Sheldon smell fish? Did Sheldon see fish? No, not yet.

No more people can be seen. No more boats can be seen. Uncle Nathan and the children were all alone on the lake.

The children and Uncle Nathan saw three white sea gulls. The sea gulls were flying in the sky.

Flap, flap, flap. The sea gulls flew away.

Uncle Nathan drove on.

Rachel hung onto her seat in the boat. They were going away from the shore. She saw the shore far away. Rachel saw the deep, blue water. She saw the waves.

Splash-sh-sh, splash-sh-sh. The waves were beside the boat.

Rachel had on her orange life jacket.

Rachel was thinking, "God will keep me safe. Uncle Nathan will drive. He wants to be safe and wise."

Rachel was happy that she went fishing. She was not afraid.

Uncle Nathan made the boat stop. Uncle Nathan wanted to sit and rock in the boat away from the shore.

"Did you see the three white sea gulls?" asked Uncle Nathan.

"Yes, I saw them!" said Rachel.

"Yes, I saw them," said Sheldon.

"Did you see the big beaks? Sea gulls like to eat fish. They watch for dead fish. They eat those fish," Uncle Nathan said. "God made sea gulls to eat dead fish and keep the lake clean."

Sheldon said, "Those white sea gulls were big."

"Yes, a sea gull is big," said Uncle Nathan. "Sometimes a sea gull swims in the water. The webs on its feet help it to swim. It rides the waves on a lake. I like to watch a sea gull ride the waves."

"Will we see a ship?" asked Rachel.

"Will we see a big, big ship?"

Uncle Nathan said, "No, we will not see a ship. A ship is much too big for this lake."

Sheldon said, "Will we see a whale? A big black whale? I want to watch a big, big whale."

"No whales," Uncle Nathan said. "A whale is much too big for this lake. God made the sea for whales. This is not a big sea. It is just a lake. But God put fish in it."

Fishing

Uncle Nathan was working while he chatted. He got a fishing line for Sheldon. Uncle Nathan put bait on the line.

"See, Sheldon? See the bait on the line? This is the way to do it. We take the rod, and we throw the bait as well as we can. Like this."

Uncle Nathan held the rod very well. He gave the top end of the rod a very quick shake. The quick shake threw much of the line away and away. The bait at the end of the line flew away and away. Then the bait sank into the water.

Uncle Nathan said, "See this reel on the rod? Next, we crank this reel."

He worked it and worked it. "We must reel the line back in. Then we can throw the line again. Then we can reel it back in. Throw and reel. Throw and reel. Maybe a fish will bite the bait while the line is coming back."

Uncle Nathan gave the rod to Sheldon. "Can you do it? Hang on to the rod. Throw the bait! Throw it as well as you can."

Rachel saw when her brother took the rod. He threw the bait, and then he began to reel the line back in.

Rachel was watching Uncle Nathan. Rachel saw when Uncle Nathan put bait on the next line.

Uncle Nathan said, "Rachel and I will use this rod. I will throw the line. Rachel can reel it back in. We want to catch a fish. We want to catch a big, long fish. If the fish is not a good size, we must put it back into the water."

Rachel was thinking, "Dear God, help us catch a fish. Help us catch a big fish."

"I hope we catch a fish!" sang Sheldon. "I hope God will help us catch a big, big fish!"

Uncle Nathan nodded. "I do too," he said.

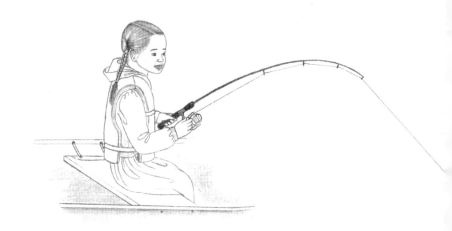

Rachel's Fish

Uncle Nathan and the children worked and waited.

Then Uncle Nathan said, "A fish! A fish is on our line!"

Rachel was very pleased. She let go of the rod. She wanted to watch Uncle Nathan bring the fish to the boat.

Uncle Nathan worked and worked.

"When will our fish reach the boat?" asked Rachel.

"I can feel it is a very big fish,"

Uncle Nathan said. "I think it is the big northern pike we want for lunch. But maybe our big fish will get away. Sometimes they do. I hope it will not get away."

The children saw the fish was coming close to the boat. Uncle Nathan was reeling it in. At last, Uncle Nathan put the long fish into the net. Then he took the net and the fish into the boat.

Sheldon sang, "We got him! We got him!"

Rachel looked at the fish in the boat. She saw it was a very big fish. The big fish had a long nose. Rachel saw its big white teeth. She was afraid of those big teeth.

Uncle Nathan said, "This fish is a northern pike. See its long nose and its teeth? I am glad this northern pike is more than three feet long. If a northern pike is between two feet and three feet, we may not keep it. It must go back into the lake. But we may keep this big fish."

Rachel was pleased. Sheldon was pleased too.

But Rachel was afraid of that big

fish. She said, "Will our fish stay
there? Will it get me?"

Uncle Nathan said, "I will not let
that fish get you, Rachel! No, no!
I will put our fish on a line. Then I
will hang the line beside the boat.
Our fish can be in the water. Then it
cannot get you."

Rachel was pleased. Then she said,
"God did help us catch a fish."

"Yes, He did," Uncle Nathan said.
He threw his line into the water
again. Then he said, "Can you catch
a fish too, Sheldon?"

Sheldon's Big Fish

Sheldon threw his line and reeled it in. He threw his line and reeled it in. He threw his line and reeled it in.

Where was Sheldon's fish? Sheldon wanted to catch a fish too.

Then Sheldon felt a tug on his line. "A fish! I got a fish too!" Sheldon said. He was very pleased.

Sheldon was feeling big, big tugs. Will the fish tug Sheldon into the lake? What very big tugs! Sheldon was afraid, but he hung on to his rod. He wanted that fish!

Rachel saw Uncle Nathan grab
Sheldon's coat. Sheldon felt Uncle
Nathan give him a very big tug. He
felt Uncle Nathan pull him back.

Sheldon was happy. Sheldon
was happy that Uncle Nathan was
hanging on to him.

Sheldon said, "A fish! I got a fish too!" He was very pleased.

Uncle Nathan was pleased too. He said, "Good for you!"

Sheldon's rod was bending to the water. Sheldon held on to his rod. He held on very well. Sheldon wanted that fish!

Then Uncle Nathan said, "I will hang on to you as long as that fish is on your line. Can you get him to the boat? Can you reel him in?"

"I will try." Sheldon began to reel in the line. He wanted to bring in that fish. He wanted it!

Uncle Nathan said, "I will watch and wait. Can you bring in your fish? Can you do it?"

Sheldon nodded. "I will work and work. I will reel in the line."

The fish was working too. It was tugging and pulling very much. It was tugging the line back that Sheldon had reeled in.

Rachel said, "Will that fish get away? Will it?"

Uncle Nathan said, "Keep trying, Sheldon. Keep on reeling it in. Hang on to that crank so the fish cannot pull the line back."

Sheldon was reeling in more line. He was hanging on to that crank very well. But it was a big job to reel in such a big fish.

Sheldon saw the fish jump up from the water. Then it went back in.

Splash!

It was very quick. But Sheldon saw his fish! Yes, he saw it for just a wee bit.

Uncle Nathan and Rachel saw that fish too. It was a northern pike. It was as big as Rachel's northern pike!

Then the fish got away! It was very sudden. The rod no longer bent to the water. Sheldon no longer felt a tug on his line. There was no fish on his line. That fish got away!

Sheldon was sad. He was very sad.

He said, "I want that fish! I want it! Why did it get away?"

Uncle Nathan said, "I am sorry that your fish got away. Sometimes they do. But can you try some more? Maybe next time you will get your fish."

Sheldon nodded. He was sad, but he said, "I will try some more."

"Reel in your line, Sheldon," Uncle Nathan said. "You will need more bait."

Uncle Nathan put on more bait. Then Sheldon threw the line. Maybe he will catch his fish yet. He wanted a fish to show Father.

Sheldon was praying, "Dear God, help me catch a fish."

Sheldon Gets a Fish

Rachel and Uncle Nathan got another fish, and Sheldon saw them bring it into the boat. They had two fish, and he did not have his first fish yet.

Sheldon was sad, but he kept on working. He threw the line and reeled it in. He threw the line and reeled it in. He threw the line and reeled it in.

After a long while, Sheldon said, "I feel a tug! I feel a fish!"

Sheldon was very happy. He said, "I think this fish is not quite as big as my first fish was. This fish can tug, but not as much."

Uncle Nathan hung onto Sheldon's coat just in case.

Sheldon was thinking, "The fish is not tugging as much. It will not tug me into the water."

Will Sheldon get this fish?

Rachel saw Sheldon reel some line in. The fish was tugging it back some, but not much.

Sheldon was reeling in more and more line. Will Sheldon get this fish? It was coming close to the boat.

At last the fish was by the boat. Will Sheldon get this fish?

Uncle Nathan put the fish into the net. Then he put the net and fish into the boat.

"Good for you!" Uncle Nathan said. "You did well."

Sheldon got his fish! He was very

pleased. May he keep it? What will Uncle Nathan say?

Uncle Nathan said, "This fish is not a northern pike, but it is the fish that I like to eat the best. This fish is a good size to keep. We will put it on the line too."

Sheldon was thinking, "Thank You, God. Thank You for helping me catch a fish."

Sheldon was happy. He was very happy! He had a fish to show Father! He had a fish for Aunt Judith to fry! He had the kind of fish that Uncle Nathan liked to eat the best.

Rachel was happy too. She was happy that Sheldon got a fish.

On the line were three fish! Three fish were on the line in the water. They had three fish to take home and eat.

Time to Go Home

After a while, Uncle Nathan and the two children had five fish.

Some fish were northern pike. Some fish were not northern pike. There were big, long fish. Some fish were not as big. The five fish were in the boat.

Uncle Nathan said, "We do not need more fish. If we want fish for lunch, it is time to go home. We must go home and clean the fish so Aunt Judith can fry them for lunch."

Uncle Nathan made the boat go. He made the boat go fast.

No other people can be seen. No other boats can be seen—just Uncle Nathan's boat and the people in it. Uncle Nathan and the children were still all alone on the lake.

Uncle Nathan drove the boat back to the dock. Uncle Nathan and the children were going home.

Sheldon felt the wind in his hair. He saw the deep water beside the boat. He saw the waves splashing by the boat.

Splash-sh-sh, splash-sh-sh.

Can Sheldon see fish this time? Can Sheldon smell the fish? Yes, he can! Rachel can too.

The fish flop at Sheldon's feet. Sheldon is very pleased. He wants to show Father the fish he got.

Sheldon had a good time, a very good time with Uncle Nathan. Sheldon was happy. He was happy that Uncle Nathan took them fishing.

Rachel was happy too. She was happy that Uncle Nathan took them fishing.

Uncle Nathan saw that the children were happy, and he was happy too.

Finding Mother and Father

When Uncle Nathan and
the children got home, Father
and Mother came to the truck.
Aunt Judith came to the truck.
Grandfather and Grandmother came
to the truck too.

"See our fish!" Sheldon said. "We
went to a lake with many fish. God
gave us fish for lunch!"

Rachel said, "See our fish! We got
five! But I do not like the big teeth."

Sheldon said, "This is the first fish I

got. My very first fish got away. But we saw it jump from the water."

Rachel said, "This fish is my first fish. Uncle Nathan said it is a northern pike."

Uncle Nathan said, "The children did well. We had a good time. But we must get to work."

Father said, "Yes, we must get to work. We need to clean the fish so Aunt Judith can fry them for lunch."

Sheldon said, "We want to watch you clean the fish."

"Clean them?" said Rachel. "Why do we clean them?"

"So we can eat them," said Father. "Watch and see."

The men cut the fish. They cut a long strip off each side. Then they took the skin off the meat. They put the meat into a big dishpan.

"What a mess!" said Rachel. "I do not want to help clean the fish. I do not want to watch. Will such fish be good to eat?"

Sheldon said, "Yes! The fried fish will be very good! God gave us the fish. It will be the best meal!"

"But what a mess!" said Rachel.

"It is a mess," said Sheldon. "But that is fine with me. I want to watch the men."

"I do not." And away she ran. Rachel ran to Mother.

Mother said, "Rachel, you may not fuss. God gave us the good fish to eat."

When all the meat was off the five fish and in a dishpan, the men put the rest of the fish into a big yellow pail.

Fried Fish for Lunch

Before long, the children smelled fried fish. The children went to watch Aunt Judith. She took the fried fish from the hot black pan on the stove. She laid the fried fish on a plate. Then she took some more fish from a dish. She laid the fish in the hot pan too.

The children can hear the fish frying in the hot pan. They can smell the fried fish.

Sheldon said, "I like that smell! I

like it very much. When can we eat lunch, Aunt Judith?"

Aunt Judith said, "Can you wait a little longer? I think we can eat before long."

"I like the smell," said Rachel. "I like the fried pike smell even more than I like fried chicken. It will be the best lunch I have had!"

Aunt Judith was pleased. "Yes, you will like the fried fish. We will all be happy for fried fish. God made good fish, and we can eat a good lunch."

The children watched Mother mash the potatoes. Mother put them in a dish. She put hot green peas in a dish too. She set the hot green peas and the potatoes on the table.

Grandmother set the cake on a plate. She put the peaches in a dish. Then she set them on the table too. Mother put purple punch in the cups.

"Good!" said Sheldon. "I think we can eat lunch."

"Yes, children," said Mother. "It is time to wash your hands. Make them very clean. Wash your cheeks too."

Sheldon said, "Yes, Mother! We will be quick."

They all sat to the table to eat lunch. Sheldon's family sat to the table. Uncle Nathan's family sat to the table too.

Uncle Nathan said, "Let us pray."

Then Uncle Nathan said, "We thank Thee, God, for this good fish. We thank Thee for giving it to us. We thank Thee for all the good things You bless us with."

Uncle Nathan said to Sheldon and Rachel, "I am happy that you came here for a meal of fried fish. Eat all you want!"

"This fried fish is so good," Sheldon said to Rachel. "I like cake and I like punch. But this fish will be the best thing for lunch."

"This fried fish is the best," Rachel said to Sheldon. "I do like fried pike even more than I like fried chicken."

Sheldon said, "I am so happy that Uncle Nathan took us fishing!"

"I am too," said Rachel. "Thank you, Uncle Nathan."

Before long, Father said to Sheldon, "You had fish three times. That is all the fish you need for lunch. Fried pike is good, but it is time for you to stop eating fish."

Sheldon obeyed. Sheldon was sorry he had to stop eating fish. He wanted to eat more of that good fish. But Sheldon was getting full. It was time to stop.

Then they all had peaches and cake.

They all had a good time chatting while they ate.

"Thank you for the good lunch," said Father and Mother.

Sheldon said, "Thank you for the very good lunch. Your fried fish is the best!"

Aunt Judith said, "We were happy to make it for you."

Uncle Nathan said to Sheldon,

"Aunt Judith did not fry all the fish for lunch. You may take the rest of the fish to Grandfather's. Maybe Grandmother can make some fried fish too."

"Thank you!" said Sheldon. "Our family will like that!"